'But I know how to stop her showing off,'
said Fred.
'Just say, "Blue custard".'
'Blue custard?' asked Tony and Tessa.
'Yes, blue custard,' said Fred.

'I went to school with Mrs Valentine.
We called her Little Dot,' said Fred.
'She was little, but she was a big
show off.'

'Her house was the best house.
Her mum was the best mum
and her cat was the best cat.
Everything she had was the best…
or so she said.'

'One day our teacher told us
about the school fair.
There was going to be a prize
for the best pudding.
Little Dot said that her pudding
would be the best.'

'I made a green jelly.
Then Little Dot came in with a big
custard tart.
It did look good, very good!'

'The puddings were put out for
people to see.
My jelly was put in the front.
It looked very good.'

'Then we all went off to play
but Little Dot came back.
She pushed my jelly out of the way
and put her custard tart in the front.'

'Everyone thought Little Dot's custard tart
would win first prize.
But she did not get a prize at all.'

'Why didn't I get first prize,' yelled
Little Dot.
'Because your custard is blue,'
said our teacher.
'What?' said Little Dot.

Little Dot went very red.
She picked up her custard tart.
It was very blue.
'Who did this?' she yelled.

Little Dot picked up her tart so fast
the custard went all over her.
Then she saw why the custard was blue.
Her pen had fallen into the custard.

After that when Little Dot was showing off
we would just say 'blue custard'.

The next day Tony and Tessa saw
Mrs Valentine.
She was washing her new car.
'My car is the best car in Wellington
Square,' she said.

'Look, I can see a mark here,'
said Tessa.
'Where?' said Mrs Valentine.
'Just here.'
'It looks like blue custard,' said Tessa.
Mrs Valentine went very, very red.

16